To all readers only if you really read this

book from the very first page,

will you understand the ending.

Acknowledgement's

To Shelley Campbell thank you for proof reading this and pointing me in the right direction.

To Philip Howkins My biggest fan thank you for all the support

To Jodie Parkin who may not forgive me for not having a perfect ending and leaving her wanting more.

To all friends and family who have shown their support

And lastly thank you to all who read this book and have a vivid imagination.

THE WRONG SIDE OF MIDNIGHT

Let me tell you the story of how it all
began,

and why I am sitting here

on the wrong side of midnight,

watching the clock and waiting!

THE LETTER

The letter reached me in early March 2022. As I rose early in the morning and peered out of the window, I discovered a fresh blanket of snow that had descended overnight. Without bothering to wash or brush my hair, I donned my dressing gown and descended the stairs to prepare a comforting cup of tea—nothing beats the warmth of tea to properly wake you up.

At the foot of the stairs, I glanced toward the front door and observed that the dedicated postman had persevered through the snow to deliver the seemingly never-ending stream of bills. They lay on the carpet, having been posted through the letterbox.

Grabbing the pile, I strolled into the kitchen, tossing them onto the table, and ambled over to the kettle to set it bubbling. No chance was I tackling any of those letters until a reliable, piping hot cuppa was cradled in my hands. With the steamy tea in tow, I sidled back to the table and took a seat.

Even then, it took a hearty gulp of the brew before I mustered the courage to crack open the first bill.

As I suspected, it was the bank, all prim and proper, reminding me (in their oh-so-formal way) that the borrowed funds were expected to be repaid in agreed-upon instalments.

They threw in the ominous warning of potential court action, threatening my credit score if I dared to stray from the agreed plan. Letting out a sigh,

I skimmed the letter across the table, muttering, "If I had the cash, why would I be begging the bank? Mental note to self: cut ties with the credit card!"

Another sip of tea proved necessary before tackling the next letter. Upon opening it, I was met with a familiar tune – the electric bill demanding its dues. Apparently, electricity is not a freebie; non-payment threatens to sever the power supply, and a court summons looms like a storm on the horizon. Letting out a deep sigh, this letter joined its banking companion on the opposite end of the table. "Memo to self: stock up on candles."

Surveying the remaining unopened letters, the daunting reality set in.

It became clear that facing them would require more than the solace of a cup of tea; a stronger elixir was in order. Yet, with the clock barely striking 10 am, it was too early for a pour of something stronger. The silver lining? An excellent excuse to procrastinate until a more appropriate hour. "Reminder to self: fetch a sizable bottle of spirits from the local shop," and, of course, the essential candles.

But hold on, how to foot the bill without resorting to the forbidden credit card? "Memo to self: reluctantly use the credit card one last time."

With the decisions made on what needed attention, I deemed it unnecessary to delve into any more bills until the evening hours.

Gathering the remaining invoices, I stacked them neatly before relocating them to the far side of the table.

However, in the process, my eyes caught a glimpse of an intriguing envelope – distinct in its cream colour, smaller and longer than the others. This piqued my curiosity.

Extracting it from the stack, I turned it over in my hands, examining it closely as if hoping for a sudden burst of X-ray vision, akin to Superman, to reveal its contents without actually opening it. Alas, there wasn't even a small transparent window for a sneak peek at the sender.

Placing it in front of me, I lifted my cuppa, taking a thoughtful sip while fixing my gaze on the enigmatic letter.

Perhaps fearing it might spontaneously unfold and start berating me, I hesitated. Naturally, no such theatrical occurrence took place, leaving me with no alternative but to muster a deep breath, seize the letter, and unravel its secrets.

Within, the missive itself boasted an opulence, crafted from fine parchment-style paper that exuded a costly aura. Prominently emblazoned at the top was the bold, elegant script of a solicitor's office in a distant city.

As my eyes initially traversed the text, I found myself more captivated by the sheer quality of the paper than the message it conveyed. Then, like a bolt from the blue, one word leapt off the page and seized my attention – "Inheritance."

WHAT???? I promptly revisited the letter, this time absorbing every word. The exquisite paper was temporarily abandoned, overshadowed by the revelation at hand.

It appeared that someone, unbeknownst to me and not even through a relative, had bequeathed their entire estate to me. Eager to unravel the details, I headed to the solicitor's office for a thorough review of the will.

However, a practical dilemma presented itself – my car was out of commission due to faulty brakes and a broken headlight. In a moment of clarity, a solution surfaced:

"Note to self, use the credit card one last time."

Shifting to a more optimistic mindset, I neatly organized the remaining bills on the table. As I reached for my cup of tea, I realized it had turned cold, prompting me to question how long I had been engrossed in the mysterious letter. While washing the cup, my mind raced with possibilities – would the inheritance clear my debts, fund a vacation, or provide a new car or a warmer home?

The anticipation of newfound wealth led me to mentally spend the money before ascertaining its form. Taking a deep breath, I reminded myself to remain composed until the details were revealed. Glancing at the clock, I noticed time slipping away. The daydreams persisted as I ascended the stairs to prepare for the day. Enter the solicitor – seizing the letter, I dialled the provided number. After a brief wait accompanied by classical music, a voice identified the company and inquired about the purpose of my call. Explaining the situation, I found myself on hold again.

Contemplating a rant, I was interrupted as the music ceased, and the solicitor introduced himself.

Confirming my identity, he informed me that the matter required an in-person meeting at their office. Suppressing the urge to unleash my frustrations, I agreed to the appointment. However, when I demanded details about reaching the office and questioned who would cover the phone bill, the solicitor's response left me speechless. He calmly stated that such matters were not their concern, ending the call abruptly. Faced with the logistical challenge of reaching the office, I weighed my options – train, bus, or the dysfunctional car? Opting for the latter, I acknowledged the need for repairs and the expense of petrol. "Note to self, use the credit card one last time."

Setting aside the bills, I resolved not to open them until the nature of my inheritance was clarified. Placing them in a drawer, I embraced the adage "out of sight, out of mind." With newfound optimism, I decided to celebrate the news. A trip to the store for a sizable bottle of spirits ensued, sans candles, and then off to the garage for the necessary car repairs.

THE CAR

As I rolled onto the garage forecourt, I spotted the mechanic and offered a friendly wave. To my surprise, he promptly lowered his head, feigning ignorance of my presence, and hurried back into his office. This peculiar behaviour left me puzzled. Nevertheless, I parked the car and approached the office, giving the door a knock and trying the handle with the intention of walking in – only to find it locked.

Glancing at my watch, I realized it was well past dinner time, raising further questions about why the door was secured. Another series of knocks followed, each more insistent than the last, but there was no response.

Resorting to a more assertive approach, I stooped down and shouted through the letterbox, insisting they open the door. After a couple of minutes and a chorus of low mumblings from inside, the door finally creaked open, revealing a young lad.

Without hesitation, I entered the office and inquired about the unusual situation. Sheepishly, the lad explained that they had both gone to the toilet.

Astonished, I questioned the logic of two people using the same toilet simultaneously, but received no reply. Turning to the head mechanic, I proceeded to explain the issues with my car and emphasized the urgency of having it fixed within the next couple of days.

The mechanic listened attentively, then took a deep breath, expressing concerns about payment this time. Drawing myself up to my full height, I demanded clarification. He proceeded to elaborate on the previous instance where my cheque had bounced, leaving him awaiting payment. Calmly, I assured him that this time, I would be settling the bill with my credit card, silently hoping that the bank wouldn't cancel it before the transaction went through. This seemed to appease him, and he agreed to proceed with the car repairs.

Leaving the vehicle in his care and promising to return in two days, I carried my lone purchase – a bottle of spirits – home. Crafting a meal for one lacked the usual joy of shared dining, so after microwaving a modest dinner, I immersed myself in music. The evening drifted by, possibly influenced by the aforementioned bottle of spirits, and glancing at the clock, I realized it was nearly midnight. With a stagger, I made my way to bed.

THE JOURNEY

As the days whisked by in a flurry, akin to the once pristine snow now reduced to brown sludge, I awoke to a cold and dismal morning. Contemplating the option of staying in bed, a sudden realization jolted me into action – today was the day I would unravel the mystery of my inheritance. With newfound determination, I swiftly prepared for the day, shaking off the lethargy that clung to me.

Hurrying downstairs, I brewed my trusty cup of tea and, seated at the table, consulted Google for the address of my destination. To my dismay, it was in a village about an hour's drive away.

No time for fretting, I needed to arrive promptly. Finishing my drink, I left the cup in the sink, donned my coat, and headed to the garage to retrieve my car. The mechanic, seemingly in a brighter mood, greeted me with a smile – perhaps anticipating payment for his work this time. He provided a list of the completed tasks, even going the extra mile to clean the car, and eagerly accepted my credit card. Following him into the office, I stood anxiously as he processed the payment.

With bated breath, I entered the code, and as the transaction was accepted, I silently thanked the powers that be. Grasping my card, I expressed gratitude and hastily departed before the whims of the bank could change.

Guided by the sat nav, I navigated out of the city and down winding country lanes. Doubts crept in as I questioned whether the navigation system was as bewildered as I felt. However, a quaint village soon came into view.

Parking in front of a shop that seemed frozen in the 16th century with its bottle-blown windows, I surveyed the surroundings.

Next to it, a closed bookshop displayed books on a table with an honesty box – a sight that would be short-lived in my bustling urban setting. Locking my car, I approached the solicitor's shop, where a bell tinkled as I opened the door. The interior indeed resembled a place from centuries past – ancient furniture, seemingly immobile staff, and an atmosphere frozen in time. Startled out of my thoughts by a tiny woman at an aged desk in the corner,

I stammered, "Err, I've come about my inheritance." Her response, "What about your inheritance?"

left me dumbfounded. Collecting myself, I clarified that I was there to discover the details.

As an internal note, I reminded myself that I had entered the twilight zone, urging myself to stay calm and exit swiftly. A resonant male voice interjected into the conversation, "Could you come this way, please? I have been expecting you." Surveying the room, I spotted an elderly white-haired man in a black suit standing by an open door. The entire setup struck me as dubious, but my desire to unravel the mystery left me with no choice but to follow him through the doorway.

As I entered the room, my eyes widened in awe. A genuine coal fire commanded one wall, a substantial desk with two chairs flanked the opposite side, bookcases adorned another wall, and a bay bottle glass window dominated the final one. He gestured towards one of the chairs, signalling for me to sit, and settled behind his desk. Opening a folder before him, he glanced at me and initiated the conversation.

THE INHERITANCE

"It would seem your cousin, eight times removed, has passed away without leaving direct heirs. Finding you has been a lengthy and arduous process on our part. Naturally, our fees will be deducted from your estate."

My mind raced, the word "estate" echoing in my thoughts. I cautiously inquired about the nature of my newfound inheritance. The man peered into the open folder before meeting my gaze.

"You have inherited your cousin's complete estate, including a manor house with all its furnishings, half an acre of land, a carriage car, and £15,000 pounds sterling. However, it took us 15 years and a substantial cost of £1000 per year, amounting to a total fee of £15,000."

Everything else is rightfully yours." He handed me the folder as I sat there, momentarily dumbfounded.

Quickly regaining my composure, I felt the need to vent my frustration. "Hold on, what do you mean my £15,000 is yours? You can't just claim it. How am I supposed to settle my credit card and debts?" The white-haired man fixed me with a steely gaze, his eyes seemingly narrowing and taking on a reddish tint, perhaps influenced by the fire's glow. In a voice that sounded deeper, he calmly asserted, "We have already deducted the fee. You'll receive a receipt at the front desk. How you manage your debts is not our concern.

Good day to you, madam." With that, he guided me out of the office to the front desk and disappeared back into the room, closing the door behind him.

The lady at the front desk handed me a receipt, showed me to the door, and that concluded the peculiar encounter.

Seated in the car, I eagerly opened the folder, diving into its contents. The realization that I now possessed a manor house, land, and even a new car filled me with satisfaction. Glancing at the address of the manor, which was entirely unfamiliar to me, I resorted to a quick Google search. To my surprise, it turned out to be situated in the middle of nowhere, an unusual locale for a manor. Despite the tempting idea of heading there immediately, the late hour discouraged me from navigating dark country lanes. Opting for prudence,

I started the car and steered back home, postponing the manor visit to the next day.

The plan was to set out early in the morning, allowing ample time to explore the estate and strategize the logistics of moving my furniture from my flat to the manor. During the journey home, I treated myself to a supper of fish and chips from the local chippy, relieved to find they accepted credit cards – the only form of payment due to concerns about counterfeit fivers.

A silent thanksgiving ensued as my card transaction was smoothly accepted, and I hastened home to savour my meal before it succumbed to the chill of the night.

A glance at the clock revealed the passage of several hours, a testament to the depth of my contemplation.

Such mental drifts were common when weighed down by heavy thoughts, and today was no exception, given the enormity of inheriting an estate. The very notion conjured images of titles, servants, and the address of "My lady!" A contented smile played on my lips, prompting an early retreat to bed to indulge in pleasant dreams of newfound wealth. The next morning, awakening naturally without reliance on an alarm, I swiftly prepared for the day. As I savoured my customary morning tea,

I compiled a list of essential items for the upcoming venture. Tape measure? YES! Kettle? YES! Milk, Sugar, Tea Bags, Cup, Spoon, YES! Satisfied, I gathered the items into a shopping bag, ready for the day ahead.

Leaving the hustle of the city and traffic snarls behind, I made good time. Consulting my watch, I was pleasantly surprised to discover it had taken only two hours to reach the nearest village to the manor's address.

Despite the temptation to inquire about the manor, I opted for the thrill of a surprise arrival. Progressing with growing excitement, I followed the sat nav's directions for the final leg of the journey.

To my utter surprise, the sat nav declared my arrival as I abruptly stopped the car. Confused, I stepped out, scanning the surroundings. Where was the manor? Where was the grand driveway? Instead, I found a large wood on one side of the country lane and a field with cows on the other.

Perplexed, I reset the sat nav, only to find it instructing a U-turn and leading me back to the same wood and cow-filled field. Determined to unravel the mystery, I decided to investigate the woods, armed with my shopping bag and a locked car. As I approached the edge of the woods, a faint path caught my attention. As I ventured along the somewhat overgrown path, I couldn't shake the thought that perhaps the field before me was the inherited land. Despite this uncertainty, I decided to press on a bit further. A clearing emerged where the trees thinned, unveiling an open space adorned with brambles and tall grass.

THE MANOR

However, the sight in the centre of this space left me utterly astounded—a colossal, hideous structure that appeared as though it belonged in a gothic horror film.

My dreams of a grand manor and a ladyship vanished, replaced by the grim reality of what seemed like the haunted house in the woods. Even in the morning sunlight, the manor was shrouded in a peculiar mist.

Undeterred, I chose to approach and scrutinize it up close. As I stood before the manor, my initial shock intensified.

Peeling paint and a rickety staircase leading to the front door did not inspire confidence in its structural integrity. Gazing upward, the tall tower attics, gargoyle stone statues, and countless faces in the windows added to the eerie ambiance.

Resigned to my fate, I cautiously ascended the stairs, half-expecting them to collapse under my weight. Surprisingly, I reached the porch unscathed, unlocking the front door with a key from my handbag. The door, made of solid oak, emitted a groan as it swung open.

Stepping into the dimly lit hall, I was met with an unexpected sight—grey shapes of varying sizes that triggered an involuntary scream.

Recoiling and making the sign of the cross, I found myself back on the porch, relieved to see that the shapes had not followed me. Squinting into the gloom, I discerned the true nature of these forms—furniture draped in dusty covers. Feeling a mix of embarrassment and gratitude that no one witnessed my initial reaction, I bravely reentered the hall, fumbling along the wall for a light switch.

After what felt like an eternity but was only seconds, my fingers found a raised round dome with a switch in the middle. Flicking it, the hall was bathed in soft light, revealing chandeliers overhead.

Turning around, I took in my surroundings—the grand staircase facing the front door, heavy curtains concealing the windows, and a newfound sense of liveability in the once dim space.

Closing the front door, I set about opening all the curtains to let sunlight flood the room, making it appear more habitable.

As I contemplated exploring the upper floors later, I decided to focus on the ground floor first.

My immediate concern was locating the kitchen for a much-needed cup of tea. The kitchen, reminiscent of medieval times with a large fireplace dominating one wall, fortunately housed an electric kettle. However, the absence of chairs prompted a mental note for a future kitchen renovation. After preparing and enjoying my cup of tea, I felt an odd sensation—eyes on me, seemingly from the staircase. Knowing I was alone, I brushed it off, yet the feeling persisted.

Placing my cup down, I resolved to explore the upper levels for my peace of mind. Reaching the top of the stairs, I found long corridors on either side. Opting to investigate the left corridor first, I opened the doors of the rooms, revealing a four-poster bed and Victorian dressing table, yet curiously lacking a bathroom. The right corridor proved to be filled with empty rooms, each void of furniture.

Perplexed by the absence of bathrooms, I noticed a slightly open door at the far end of the corridor, blending seamlessly with the panelling.

Intrigued, I approached the door and tried to open it, only to discover it resisted my efforts. There was something eerie about it, and the tingling sensation up my spine intensified.

Despite my efforts, the door remained firmly shut, prompting me to consider tools from the outbuildings seen through a window. Noting to myself not to emulate the Hulk without his strength, I retraced my steps, descended the stairs, and headed to the back door leading to the rear of the house.

Using the keys, I attempted to unlock the door, facing some resistance. Finally opening it, the door emitted a groan, much like its counterpart at the front. Outside, I found three outbuildings, with the largest resembling a barn. Hoping they held useful items, I approached and pulled on one of the double doors...

I'm not sure if it was just good sense prevailing or an inexplicable force guiding me, but for whatever reason, I instinctively pulled the door to the left.

It turned out to be a fortunate decision because the entire door, complete with hinges, crashed forward. If I hadn't moved in time, it would have flattened me. Standing there, still trembling, I questioned the wisdom of venturing alone.

What if something went wrong? A mental note to myself: avoid unnecessary risks and be prepared to run for safety if things seem suspicious.

Now that the door was open, I cautiously stepped onto the fallen debris, maintaining a safe distance from the remaining door, in case it decided to follow its counterpart. As

I peered into the dilapidated structure, I hesitated to enter. The roof had mostly collapsed, leaving a chaotic mix of rubble and beams. In the midst of it all, I discerned a mysterious object covered in dirt. It took a moment for my eyes to focus, and when they did, disbelief washed over me. There it was—an eighteenth-century hearse.

How unexpected and oddly fitting for this eerie place. It seemed I had inherited a carriage car instead of a sleek sports car. Oh well, maybe I could list it online for sale, under the condition of buyer collection.

Moving on to the next building, I discovered it lacked a door altogether, having fallen off long ago. Despite the missing door, the roof remained intact. As I cautiously entered, my eyes adjusted to the gloom, revealing tools on a table against the nearest wall. Gathering my courage, I approached and picked up a corroded and rusty object, which turned out to be a wrench. Disheartened, I realized these tools were beyond use. Discarding the useless tool, I left the building and moved on to the last one. Was it worth checking its interior?

The door proved unyielding, and the grimy windows made it challenging to peer inside. Squinting against the sunlight, I managed to glimpse an empty room.

Returning to the main house, I pondered my options. With the late afternoon setting in, I decided to call it a day and return tomorrow. I gathered my belongings, locked the back door, and made my way to the hall. While heading for the front door, I caught a fleeting glimpse of someone at the top of the stairs. A second glance revealed nothing, but the unsettling feeling lingered. It was time to leave.

Opening the front door, I turned off the lights, leaving the curtains open to avoid surprises tomorrow.

As I locked the front door, I descended the steps with a sense of relief. Glancing at the darkening sky, I realized the sun had already set, and dusk had settled in. Shaking my head, I headed through the woods to locate my car. When I finally found it, the darkness had fully enveloped the surroundings. Unlocking the door, I hastily got in and secured the lock. A strange unease lingered, and without any apparent reason, the hairs on the back of my neck stood on end.

Pulling my coat tighter, I fastened the seat belt, started the engine, and decided to leave swiftly. Just as the car began to move, a loud bellowing echoed from the field to the left. A mental note to self: never venture into that field with the seemingly mad cows.

The return journey to civilization proved uneventful, and I made excellent time with surprisingly little traffic. Upon reaching my reliable flat, I securely locked up the car and hurried inside, relishing the familiar comforts of home. Igniting the fireplace and settling down with a well-deserved glass of spirits, I mulled over my choices.

Did I truly want to revisit that desolate place? If not, the mystery behind that door would remain forever unknown, potentially hiding family heirlooms that I wouldn't want to miss out on discovering. Yet, what if there was nothing of value, or worse, if the floor crumbled beneath me, leading to an uncertain fate? So many questions flooded my mind, prompting me to sleep on the matter and make a decision upon waking.

Upon opening my eyes, I found myself not in my bed but on the sofa in front of the fireplace. Clearly, fatigue had overtaken me more than I realized. Glancing out the window, I observed storm clouds looming overhead, their ominous dark grey hue solidifying my resolve.

There was no way I would venture back to that place in the midst of a storm, especially through those eerie woods. Mental note to self: use the credit card one last time to restock on booze; a trip to the shop was in order.

Rushing to the corner shop, I swiftly gathered a few essentials, including candles (one never knows when they might be needed), a tin of oil, a hammer, and two bottles of spirits.

Figuring it was my last chance to use the credit card before deciding not to rely on it anymore, I held my breath as I handed over the card and entered the number. To my relief, it was accepted, and I hurriedly left before it could change its mind. Imagining the bank manager scrambling to stop the card, I half-expected them to be waiting at my door, but it was quiet.

Engaging in chores like cleaning, washing, drying, and ironing, I passed the day swiftly. As evening fell, the storm raged outside, but I found solace in the warmth of my cozy flat.

Switching on the side lamps, I prepared supper and returned to the living room to savour it in front of the fire. After finishing my meal and tidying up,

I settled back on the sofa with my trusted bottle of spirits and glass, contemplating my next move. The Victorian funeral car in the garage crossed my mind; perhaps it held some value. Should I sell it online now? The thought of potential buyers exploring the garage in my absence made me wary, although the state of the garage roof provided some reassurance.

Deciding to wait until I had thoroughly examined everything in the house, I resolved to make one last visit, hoping there were no more unwelcome surprises. On that note, I extinguished the fire, left my glass in the kitchen, and headed to bed.

I awoke to bright sunlight streaming through the window, relieved to see no signs of rain. Swiftly getting ready, I made a cup of tea, gathered my necessities into a bag, and, satisfied that I had everything short of the kitchen sink, donned my coat and hurried out the door, hoping for a day of sunshine and no unpleasant surprises.

Stepping into my car and igniting the engine, a decision crystallized in my mind – if possible, I would spend the night at my new manor to grasp its ambiance. A swift detour to the local shop for sustenance became a priority.

Racing into the shop and snatching a couple of pot noodles, I approached the counter, assuming my most innocent expression, and handed over cash, bypassing the credit card this time. With the payment accepted, I mentally noted, "DO NOT USE AGAIN."

The drive unfolded uneventfully, and the traffic was mercifully light, allowing me to make good time. Around 11 am, I reached the woods where the sun still cast its warmth. Meandering through the trees, I pondered the elusive real driveway and resolved to locate it soon; after all, navigating the woods with furniture in tow was an impractical notion. As I entered the clearing, there stood the imposing house, prompting a double take. The realization that such a monstrosity was now mine struck me anew. Sighing deeply, I extracted the key from my bag and approached the precarious stairs leading to the door.

They appeared even more precarious today, so I hugged the edge and ascended cautiously, half-expecting a surprise attack upon reaching the porch. However, only silence greeted me. With the key, I opened the front door and ventured inside.

The hall, bathed in light upon flicking the switch, reassured me of its emptiness. Proceeding to the kitchen, I set the kettle on and unpacked my belongings, contemplating my next move after the cuppa. It dawned on me that, despite inspecting the upstairs, the mysteries of the downstairs still lingered. Standing at the kitchen door leading to the hall, I surveyed the doors leading off it, sparking curiosity about what lay behind each one. Returning to the kitchen, I made my cuppa and, returning to the hall, sat down.

As I sat there, doubts crept into my mind. Was I being foolish? Did I truly want to move into this house? My inner voice replied with a resounding "no way," suggesting putting it up for sale; surely, someone eccentric would be eager to purchase it. Despite this thought, I recognized the need to scrutinize every room, as there might be hidden treasures behind one of those doors.

With my cup in hand, I resolved to start by checking the rooms leading off the hall, hoping to find the elusive bathroom. Carrying my cup, I approached the first door and turned the handle. To my surprise, it swung open effortlessly, revealing a room steeped in gloom.

I hastened to the window and drew back the curtains, flooding the room with light. It appeared to be a massive living room, adorned with a fireplace dominating one wall and a crest of arms engraved above the mantel, oddly intriguing even if it felt like something out of the twilight zone. Observing that the furniture was draped in dust cloths, I decided against unveiling them for now. Moving on to the next door,

I opened it to a similar gloomy scene. Again, I opened the curtains to unveil a different room, this time housing a grand piano beneath its dust cover. The glint of potential wealth crossed my mind, and the idea of consulting a dealer to assess the furniture's worth seemed appealing. On this notion, I proceeded to explore the rest of the downstairs.

Each room I explored on the upper floor revealed only covered furniture, no treasures in sight, but the potential value of the furniture lingered in my thoughts. "Note to self: contact a dealer." Another reminder popped up, "Note to self: find the main driveway first." After concluding the downstairs exploration, I placed my cup in the kitchen, gathered my few tools, flashlight, and tin of oil, ready to ascend.

With purpose in my stride, I hastened to the slightly ajar door at the far end of the corridor. Without bothering to tug at the door, I removed the lid from the tin of oil and poured it over the hinges. As the instructions advised, I left it for five minutes, utilizing the time to gaze through the corridor's window overlooking what was once the garden—now an overgrown mess with the tops of ruined sheds and garages peeking through the weeds and grass.

Returning to the door, I gently tugged, but it resisted. Debating whether to wait a little longer or wield my trusty hammer, I chose the latter, delivering a resounding blow to all three hinges in a burst of frustration. This, unfortunately, caused the door to slam shut, eliciting a scream of rage. Determined, I decided on one final attempt and vowed to break it down with my hammer if it didn't yield. Grabbing the handle, I turned it, pulled hard, and the door swung open, propelling me backward to the floor. Bewildered, I stood up, nursing my sore areas, and peered into the darkness beyond. I switched on my bright torch, revealing a stairway leading upward.

With trepidation, I ascended, half-expecting the bogeyman to appear. Standing at the top, I surveyed two long corridors, much like the lower floors.

My torch illuminated boarded-up windows, a puzzling discovery. Venturing into the first room on the left, I found it empty, devoid of even a fireplace, with its window boarded up.

The pattern continued in the other rooms of that corridor.

Moving to the right corridor, the same boarded-up windows and empty rooms persisted. The strangeness of the situation puzzled me—why was this floor sealed off, and why were the windows all boarded up? It felt eerie. Sighing, I retraced my steps to the top of the stairs. The prospect of the uppermost stairs intrigued me, and I wondered if I detected movement in the darkness. Dismissing it as imagination, I climbed slowly, arriving at a closed door.

Assuming it led to the attic, I turned the handle and pushed, met with resistance. After exerting more force, the door creaked open, revealing another long corridor stretching in both directions.

My torch illuminated the dark expanse, leaving me wondering about the countless rooms in this vast space. The idea of transforming the place into apartments crossed my mind, promising potential profit. I could make a killing! Food for thought indeed.

"Note to self: find the driveway first; how will the workers renovate without access?" Surveying the corridors, I opt to explore the right side first, mirroring the layout of the floor below, complete with boarded-up windows and three mysterious doors.

The first door groans open under my touch, revealing a room stacked with boxes. A small boarded-up window fails to illuminate the room, but I explore a few boxes, finding old papers and books. Recognizing it as a storage room, I decide to return later for a thorough investigation.

The subsequent door reveals an empty room, confirming my diminishing hopes of discovering hidden treasures. The last door, too, disappoints with emptiness.

Suddenly, a realization strikes me—the downstairs corridor had four rooms on each side, while this floor only has three. I backtrack, scanning the corridor for hidden doors or outlines. Frustrated, I notice bulb sockets without bulbs in the ceiling. "Note to self: get bulbs;" another reminder not to use the credit card fills my thoughts.

Desperate to continue, I succumb to a final credit card use.

In my self-conversation, I inadvertently reach the other side of the corridor and stand puzzled by the door leading downstairs. Progressing down the left corridor, I open three more empty rooms, puzzled by the discrepancy.

As I approach the fourth door, it silently swings open, revealing a room with a made-up bed, open curtains, and a fresh, lived-in appearance. Unease creeps in; I retreat, close the door, and try to rationalize the surreal experience.

Upon a second glance, the room still appears recently used. The hair on my neck rises, and an unsettling feeling intensifies. Hastily, I close the door, sprint down the stairs, collect my belongings, switch off the lights, and flee the house.

The creaky porch steps don't hinder my escape until I reach my car. Overwhelmed, I lock myself in, trying to comprehend the situation. Who was living in my house, and how did they gain access? The absence of broken windows suggests they have a key, a disconcerting thought. Memories of feeling watched and the elusive hidden door resurface. Closing my eyes, I inhale deeply, attempting to regain composure.

Checking the time, it's past four in the afternoon. Hours have slipped away during my unsettling exploration of the upper floors.

One firm thought dominates my mind—I won't be spending the night in that house.

Twisting the key in the ignition, I slammed the car into gear and sped away from the manor, my mind refusing to dwell on the eerie events that had transpired. My sole focus became the pressing need for a stiff drink, the stiffer, the better. Arriving at the corner shop, I navigated instinctively to the booze aisle, a resolute "sod the credit card, my need is greater" echoing in my mind. Grabbing a couple of bottles, I added a third for good measure, then made my way to the freezer for ready meals, and finally, to the bulbs, securing four of them. At the counter, I handed over the credit card, offering a sweet smile without a prayer crossing my lips as I paid for my items. Returning to the car, I hopped in and drove home, feeling a slight improvement in my spirits.

Sleep proved elusive; my brain churned with questions and scenarios. The night unfolded on the sofa, with me consuming booze and attempting to decipher the enigma unfolding at the manor.

Replaying recent events in my mind, I pondered the unsettling possibility of someone else inhabiting my house. Should I involve the police? But what evidence did I have? The logical part of me argued against such a move; they would likely dismiss me as crazy without concrete proof. Maybe consulting the lawyers could shed light, but considering their past attempts to locate me, it seemed unlikely they had discovered someone else in the manor.

Observing the clock, I realized it was well past 4 am. Not only had I forgotten to have supper, but I also had polished off two bottles of booze, the last bottle standing alone beside the empty ones.

Recognizing my unfit state to drive in the morning and questioning my desire to return to the manor, a nagging voice reminded me of the practicality of paying bills. Sighing deeply, I opted to delve into the history of the house. Googling its name, I uncovered news articles dating back years. The manor, constructed in the early 1800s, had initially belonged to a family who gradually sold off the surrounding land. The last owner, without heirs, passed away, leaving the property abandoned.

One particular article seized my attention, chronicling strange sightings over the years—lights flickering in empty rooms, shadows passing by windows, and even reports of music, as if a ball were in progress. Early police investigations yielded no evidence, leading people to dub the manor as haunted, effectively steering clear of it. Despite a few additional articles reiterating the haunted status, I rubbed my eyes wearily and powered down the internet, realizing I had unwittingly become the owner of a notorious haunted house avoided by all.

Cracking open the last bottle and replenishing my glass, I pondered the recent turn of events. What if the manor wasn't haunted? What if someone had consistently resided there after the owner's demise? Considering the evidence I had witnessed, it seemed plausible. But who could it be? An old servant, a companion to the former owner? Determined to unravel the mystery, I embraced my inner detective; after all, it was my house, and I wasn't entertaining the idea of free lodgers. Downing the last drops of the bottle, I let my mind wander, eventually succumbing to an unconscious state. When I regained my senses, the sun was already illuminating the outside world. Groaning, I decided to postpone the day, stumbling upstairs to bed. Sleep claimed me swiftly, and I didn't wake until the following day.

Awakening to the sound of rain tapping on the window, my initial inclination was to stay in bed. After all, the manor wasn't going anywhere. However, practicality nudged me; I needed a plan of action. Gearing up for the day, I washed, dressed, and went downstairs.

Contemplating my first steps, I realized pepper spray should be a priority. After a search through the drawers, I located two tins and stowed them in my bag. One last check around, ensuring nothing was forgotten, and I closed the front door, heading to the car.

Making good time, I arrived at the forest a little after nine am. The sky was overcast, hinting at an impending storm—just what I needed. Locking the car, I noticed an old man by the field fence, appearing to watch me intently. Intrigued, I approached and attempted to glean information.

Despite my inquiries, he responded with silence, merely pointing down the lane towards the manor's driveway. As he retreated into the field, I continued down the lane and discovered a massive gate, wide open. Driving through, I found the overgrown but passable driveway leading straight to the manor. Grinning to myself, I ascended the stairs to the door without concern for locking car or the dodgy steps.

Retrieving the keys, I flung the door open, exclaiming, "Honey, I'm home!" – a playful warning to any potential intruders.

Carrying essentials to the kitchen, I resisted the temptation for a cuppa, focusing on exploring and uncovering any hidden doors. Stowing necessary items in my pockets, I ascended directly to the third floor.

Replacing bulbs and flooding the corridor with light, I scrutinized the walls, discovering a faint line at the far end. After a careful examination, I sensed a click, and the wall yielded, revealing a dark passage.

Holding my pepper spray like a weapon, I approached the staircase, torch in hand. As I ascended, the realization dawned: the corridor extended endlessly. Stepping forward, something brushed my forehead, and in an instant, my surroundings shifted. A scream escaped me as I collided with a solid object, sending me into a dizzying fall. My last conscious thought was a silent gratitude to the powers that be—I was falling forward, not backward down the stairs. However, I succumbed to unconsciousness before colliding with the floor.

Gradually regaining awareness, I groaned as my hand instinctively reached for my head. Wait, what? This couldn't be right! My hand met something soft where my head should be. Opening my eyes, I found myself in an unfamiliar room. A bandage was wrapped around my head. Confusion swept over me. How had I ended up here, lying on a bed in what seemed like the 1800s? And what was that ticking sound?

With effort, I sat up, taking in the surroundings. A fire burned in the grate, and everything exuded an antiquated charm. As I steadied myself, the room spun briefly. I forced myself to walk toward the fireplace, confirming the reality of a blazing fire. Glancing down, I realized I was wearing an old-fashioned nightgown.

My head throbbed, and as I surveyed the room in bewilderment, the distinct sound of footsteps halted outside the door.

The doorknob turned slowly, and the door creaked open, revealing a diminutive woman in period attire. Before I could utter a word, she spoke, expressing concern about my head injury and how lucky it was that someone named Bess had found me.

She assured me they would take care of me and left to fetch hot broth.

Dumbfounded, I was left with a flood of questions. Who was Bess, and why was she in my house? Attempting to unravel the mystery, I opened my mouth to speak, but the woman returned, gently guiding me back to bed. She reassured me with soothing words and vanished, closing the door behind her.

I sat up abruptly; confusion and anxiety gripped me. What had transpired? Where was I?

I glanced at the window, expecting daylight, but it was pitch-dark outside. How long had I been unconscious? The loud ticking continued, and upon closer inspection, I identified a great grandfather clock in the corner. Squinting, I discerned the time: 12:04 AM. I should have been on the other side of midnight—it should be 12:04 PM.

Terrified and bewildered, I resisted the urge to cry for help, fearing the unknown woman's return. Unable to endure the uncertainty, I needed to find my clothes and discover where I was. The room was dimly lit by the fire, allowing me to spot my clothes on a chair.

Dressing silently, I approached the door, feeling along the wall for a light switch. To my surprise, there was none. Desperation growing, I discovered an old lamp with a candle and wicks by the dressing table.

Picking up the lamp and wick, I ignited it at the fire, providing some light. Eager to escape, I gently opened the door, peering cautiously in both directions. The corridor, lit by spaced lamps, looked oddly familiar. Going to a window, I observed a well-kept back garden illuminated by the full moon. The painted white sheds, a mowed lawn, and flower beds hinted at an eerily picturesque scene.

Yet again, that persistent feeling lingered— like a vague memory I had encountered this scene before, but not exactly the same. After scanning the area, I opted to go left and explore where it led. At the end, I discovered a flight of stairs descending and another corridor branching off to the left. Something attempted to jog my memory, but it remained elusive, akin to those moments in a dream where recollection slips through your grasp upon waking. Determining to descend the stairs, I could hear faint sounds emanating from the left, and the front door lay ahead.

Hastening down the final steps, I headed for the front door, grappling with disbelief.

My luck ran out as I grasped the handle— locked! Well, what else should I have expected? No one leaves their door unlocked in the early hours of the morning.

A sense of bewilderment enveloped me as I pondered my next move. I couldn't escape this way, and panic began to well up. Surveying my surroundings, I found myself in a hall adorned with furniture along one side. Closing my eyes, I resisted the unsettling realization my brain was attempting to convey.

Ignoring the nagging thoughts, I reopened my eyes and glanced to the right. A faint light emanated from under a door through an archway, leading to another corridor with doors leading off. Deep down, I knew where this door led, an awareness I had always possessed but refused to acknowledge. Steeling myself, I turned the handle, pushing the door inward.

Warmth embraced me from the fireplace dominating the wall, while the once-vacant table now bore pots and vegetables, a spit roasting some animal over the fire. Two heads turned to face me as I stood in the doorway. All I heard were the words "What in the world" before I spun around, making a swift retreat back up the stairs. Regrettably, I could already discern someone following me. With my heart pounding, I sprinted up the stairs to the room I had come from.

However, in the midst of panic, I struggled to recall which room it was. As I paused at the top of the stairs, deliberating whether to turn left or right down the corridors, a gentle hand took hold of my arm.

Glancing around, the woman from downstairs had joined me on the landing. "Where be ye going?" she asked in an accent I could scarcely understand. "Ye be the death of us poor staff if the missus comes back and finds ye have disappeared. What would we do then?"

Gently but firmly tugging my arm, she led me back to the room I had emerged from, seating me on the bed. She fetched my nightgown and returned, urging me to get back into bed before I caught a chill. "And I think we will have to have the doctor in to see you in the morning; this is a strange going on without a doubt."

Shaking her head and tutting, she examined my clothes. "Where be ye getting those strange clothes from? I have never seen the like of them before." Mumbling under my breath, I allowed her to help me undress, and she appeared particularly intrigued by the zip on my top. Even in my predicament, I couldn't help but smile at her bewildered expression.

After assisting me back into bed for the second time that night, she picked up my clothes and headed to leave the room. "Wait," I called. She stopped and turned around. "Leave the clothes. Put them over there on that chair."

She hesitated, eyeing me and the clothes in her hands. "But these be strange things, and missus will want to see them when she returns." "NO!" I shouted, making her jump. "Just do as I said. Put them over there. I will discuss it in the morning. Now go; I am tired and wish to sleep."

Tutting again and shaking her head, she placed the clothes on the chair and left the room, closing the door behind her. A sigh of relief escaped me once she had gone. Seated on the bed, I contemplated my next move, realizing I had none. I was trapped here, but how? Revisiting my movements from the time I left home until I hit my head on the door frame—something I now knew had occurred—nothing made any sense. Unless I was knocked out longer than I thought. No, that didn't make sense; it still failed to explain how I got here. Could it be possible, my God, that I had traversed through time to an earlier period?

But how? Did the house slip back in time at a certain hour? Was that the reason so many reported seeing lights and hearing music in the early morning hours? I felt like I was teetering on the edge of madness, but I knew I had to remain calm if I had any hope of returning to my own time. Should I descend back down and engage in conversation to seek clues about what had happened? No, that wouldn't work; they'd likely summon the doctor immediately and have me locked away! I looked around for my bag—damn, I had left it in the kitchen earlier, and my phone was inside. However, I doubted if my phone would function in a different time zone. "Think, stay calm; you can do this," I reassured myself. "What reassurance?" my inner voice mocked me. "Stuck in some other dimension, goodness knows where," the inner voice continued, echoing my sense of despair. Flipping heck, why hadn't I informed anyone about my visit here? The voice replied, "Perhaps because there was no one you could tell!" As I pondered, I realized my inner voice was right—I had no one to tell. Brought up in care, I had never formed any close connections and was content to be alone. While others played outside, I'd immerse myself in a good book. That mindset had carried me through life, and no one would notice my absence. No friends, no family; there was no one to miss me, apart from the bank. Would they report me missing? I doubted it. They'd likely be pleased their credit card had stopped being used. Finally, the stark reality hit—I was on my own, and no one was coming to my rescue. If I were to escape this predicament, I would have to do it on my own. As I sat there, something tried to break through my train of thought. The clock—why had I not considered it before? I hadn't heard it when I first entered the house, so why was it audible now? It could be merely because it belonged to this time zone, or perhaps I hadn't entered the room where it was earlier. Conversations with oneself could be irksome, but it was my method of arriving at a logical explanation. It made sense when I considered it; if it was the clock, then at some point, it might propel the house back into the future. That had to be the answer; there was no other explanation. "Okay, so what now?" I asked myself. "Just sit here and wait? What if nothing happens? What then? Attempt to acclimate to this time zone? What if I become like my distant cousin? What if I am my distant cousin? Oh, damn, don't think about that. Just sit here quietly and see what happens."

The End?